REUNION

To my grandmother, Georgiana,
and my grandfather, Andy,
who saved the pictures
and told the stories

GREEN TIGER PRESS
Simon & Schuster Building, Rockefeller Center
1230 Avenue of the Americas, New York, New York 10020
Copyright © 1994 by Roger Essley
All rights reserved including the right of reproduction
in whole or in part in any form.
GREEN TIGER PRESS is an imprint of Simon & Schuster.
The text for this book is set in 14 point Palatino.
The illustrations were done in pastels and conte crayon.
Manufactured in the United States of America

10 9 8 7 6 5 4 3 2 1

Library of Congress Cataloging-in-Publication Data
Essley, Roger. Reunion / by Roger Essley.
p. cm. Summary: While looking at a box of faded
old photographs at his grandmother's summer cottage,
Jon finds he has become part of the pictures.
[1. Photographs—Fiction. 2. Space and time—Fiction.]
I. Title. PZ7.E7475Pau 1994 [E]—dc20 93-12035 CIP
ISBN: 0-671-86722-9

REUNION

BY ROGER ESSLEY

GREEN TIGER PRESS
Published by Simon & Schuster
New York   London   Toronto   Sydney
Tokyo   Singapore

Slap! Jon saw only ripples as the fish slipped back into the water. He sighed as he left the dock, remembering that his week at his grandmother's cottage was almost over.

Letting the screen door of the cottage bang behind him, Jon found his grandmother dusting the old photographs that hung above the couch. "The lake is as peaceful today, and the sky almost as blue, as summers when I was a girl," she said.

Jon wondered what it was his grandmother remembered so fondly about those old days when the people in those photographs were still alive. Everything in them looked so gloomy and gray.

"I'm going up for a little nap," said his grandmother, handing him a dented tin box. "You might enjoy looking through this, Jon."

Jon settled on the couch and opened the box. Inside he found a tattered old baseball, a kite string, a pocketknife, a broken harmonica, and a small photo album. On the album's cover was written *Paul's Fantastic Photos—1915*. Jon opened the book. "More gloomy gray pictures," he muttered to himself as he turned the pages.

Jon thought he heard laughter behind him. Glancing around, he noticed one of the pictures on the wall was tilted. He peered at the photograph of a boy sitting by a lily pond. Under the picture was written—*Paul, July 1915*. The clocks his grandmother wound each night seemed to be ticking more slowly.

Jon thought he heard a faint voice calling, "Hide and seek. You're it!" Jon leaned toward the picture, and then blinked. The boy sitting by the pond had disappeared!

"Wait!" called Jon, climbing up on the couch. From far-away he heard the lamp crash as he fell.

Jon found himself sprawled among lily pads. "I really have fallen into that old gray picture," he said to himself. And now he was gray, too! The air was still and smelled stuffy, like things stored in an old attic trunk.

Suddenly a boy squirmed out of the bushes. Jon recognized Paul's solemn face from the old photo. "You'd better not let Aunt Ruth catch you bathing in her lily pond," Paul called. Then the serious look vanished and Paul was laughing.

"Wow," said Jon, "I've never been *in* a picture before, but I guess *you're*
stuck in this stuffy old place. Do you get used to everything being gray?"

"Gray—is that all you see?" asked Paul.

Jon was trying to figure out what Paul meant when he suddenly remembered the photo album he still clutched in his hand. "Is this yours?" he asked.

"Yes," answered Paul. "Do you like my pictures?"

Jon opened the album, trying to think of something polite to say about the gloomy pictures. "They're nice I guess. . . ." he mumbled.

"I'll tell you a secret," said Paul. "Pictures can come to life. Sometimes they're just waiting for the right person to come along and really look at them."

Jon looked at several pictures, wondering what he was supposed to see.

"It takes a little practice," said Paul. A faded picture of a frozen lake caught Jon's attention. "Now look at it really closely," urged Paul.

Suddenly Jon saw snow blowing across the ice! A gust of fresh cold wind tore the picture from the album. Reaching for it, he slipped. He scrambled clumsily to his feet—in the middle of the lake.

Echoing from the gray shore came a crashing noise. Jon saw horses and a wagon plunging down the snowy slope toward the lake.

Out onto the ice they came, right toward him. The horses pulled up with a jerk. "Everyone out!" shouted the driver.

Paul was the first to climb down. "We're going to cut the ice," he said to Jon. "You can help if you want." Jon and Paul helped clear and mark lines on the ice. Then the cutting began.

As they rode toward shore atop the load of ice blocks, Jon asked, "What's this ice for?"

"For the icebox next summer, of course," said Paul. When darkness fell, everyone gathered around a bonfire, and Paul said, "Now comes the best part."

Stew and spiced cider steamed on the fire. Jon and Paul both had seconds. Later as the skaters glided into the firelight, then faded into the darkness, Paul told Jon about them.

"That's Uncle Jack. He hates horses and farm work, so he lives in town. Look at Mom. She's the best skater of all. Once she skated around the whole lake."

The moon was setting when Paul said, "There's a picture of our farm you might like to see." In the fading firelight Jon found a picture of a farmhouse. The car in front of the house caught his attention. The sun flashed off its windshield.

Jon stood blinking in the farmyard. There was no one in sight.

As Jon approached the funny-looking car, Paul stood up in the back seat.

"This is Uncle Jack's new automobile," said Paul proudly, climbing into the front seat. "He says it's as fast as a horse and doesn't kick. Hop in." While Paul turned the steering wheel this way and that, and Jon tried out the controls, the car suddenly started rolling down the hill.

Jon yelled, "Hit the brakes!"

Paul, trying to steer, shouted, "The what?"

They bounced off the road, heading straight for a pond. Jon looked
around frantically. He pulled a lever. The car lurched and skidded.

Jon and Paul fell forward as the car slid to a stop at the edge of the pond. They stared at each other—and burst out laughing.

Then someone shouted from the house, and Paul said to Jon, "You'd better go."

"Yes, I guess I should get back to my grandmother's cottage," said Jon, "but how?"

Paul thought a moment and said, "Row."

Grown-ups were running toward the car as Jon found a picture of several row-boats tied to a dock.

Jon set off in the rowboat. He didn't see any cottages, but in the misty silence he saw large birds skimming the lake. A raccoon waded, hunting crayfish. Several deer watched him pass.

Jon thought he glimpsed a hint of blue sky above the mist. He was rounding a point when suddenly he knew this place. Someday his grandmother's cottage would stand on this beautiful wooded point. Ahead he saw a rowboat pulled up onshore, and kids swimming.

Paul waved and said, "There's not much time left. I want to take a picture." One of the kids aimed Paul's box camera and took everyone's picture. Someone yelled, "Last one in's a rotten egg!"

That night Jon took Paul's album to bed with him.
On the last page was a picture Jon hadn't seen before.
Under it was written *Jon's first visit*.